ANCHOR
BOOKS

# *SINISTER SMILES*

Edited by

Kelly Oliver

First published in Great Britain in 2002 by
ANCHOR BOOKS
Remus House,
Coltsfoot Drive,
Peterborough, PE2 9JX
Telephone  (01733) 898102

HB ISBN 1 85930 854 6
SB ISBN 1 85930 859 7

# *FOREWORD*

Anchor Books is a small press, established in 1992, with the aim of promoting readable poetry to as wide an audience as possible.

We hope to establish an outlet for writers of poetry who may have struggled to see their work in print.

The poems presented here have been selected from many entries. Editing proved to be a difficult task and as the Editor, the final selection was mine.

I trust this selection will delight and please the authors and all those who enjoy reading poetry.

Kelly Oliver
Editor

Where the Grey Lady.
On page 66.
Written by:-

Susan Carole Roberts.

# CONTENTS

## COULD IT BE

I suppose I'll have to make it,
Though it's hard for me to take it,
I've just lost another relative today,
There is nothing can be surer,
Than my life is so much poorer,
For the loss of everyone who's passed away,
But when no amount of crying,
Ever helps the dead or dying,
I am forced to ask myself if it could be,
That I never cried for mother,
Poor dear father, sister, brother,
That I cried for no one other than poor me.

*Matthew L Burns*

## THEY'VE GOT BENDY

'They've got Bendy,' screamed Kurly the kiwi fruit, as a hand lifted a banana from the fruit bowl.

'Don't worry about me,' laughed Bendy, 'this is what I've been waiting for.'

The hand peeled Bendy. Kurly stifled a tear and watched his friend smile as he approached a ravenous mouth . . .

*Francis McFaul*

## THE BLACK CAT

The black cat sat on the fence staring at the old woman in her rocking chair.

It would only eat food from her hands. She could see into the future.

Her heart was weak so she died. Her children were by her side.

The black cat was never seen again.

*Jean Paisley*

## THE CHASE

The initial sound of rhythmic pounding, decreased the distance between them. Straining, he pushed to his limits in a last attempt to widen the gap. Feeling their hot moist breath as they brushed past, tails wagging triumphantly, as yet again, it was the dogs who won the race back home.

*Pam Wettstein*

## DEATH-TRAP

Teetering upon worlds, deadliest verge,
completely lost, submerged within life's
stormy endless rhythm.
Tremendous noise, so loud, bursts
unprotected eardrums, demons, screaming
moaning, groaning.
Yet quiet secrets, transports my confused
brain towards elusive daydreams.
Blinking both eyes, facing towards where
I want to go . . .
The other side of this road.

*Ann Hathaway*

## AFTER THE DINOSAURS CAME

Our creator wasn't too happy with man,
when he started protecting endangered species from becoming extinct.
They thought they were doing the right thing,
but you see, our creator wanted the animal kingdom to evolve.
How could it with man always interfering.

*Dawna Mechelle*

# THE MIRACLE

It was love at first sight and we married.
For three years it was heaven, now this
catastrophe threatened our lives.
She was in pain, I could do nothing to help.
She clung to my hand,
suddenly it was all over.
We held our first baby
in our arms.

*Gladys Baillie*

## WHAT THE EYE DOES NOT SEE . . .

She dialled a wrong number. He answered. They talked. He dialled 1471. They talked again. Often. They agreed to meet outside the station at seven. She arrived early and waited. He arrived promptly but couldn't see her. At eight they walked away in opposite directions, led by their guide dogs.

*Jennifer Bailey*

## THE JOURNEY'S END

The journey had seemed endless but, with euphoria, she could see in the distance her destination. Not long now. She was exhausted, and the anticipation of her arrival was overwhelming. Familiar faces she had thought long dead beckoned her. She joined them gladly. Her bereaved family bade farewell with sadness.

*Gillian Edge*

## DANGEROUS MOMENTS

River Picnic, oars row
Suddenly, head o'er heels
Into depths go.
Embarrassed, saved by branching tree.

'Dangers, risks, on river water'
Words my recent speech.
Hoping ne'er to hear ever
'Practise what you preach'.

*Ivy Lott*

# A TIME OF CHANGE

As the blood-curdling scream pieced the night air,
The girl's mother ran into the room.
'What's wrong?'
The girl's face was ghost-like white, her eyes wide with fear.
'It's horrible, disgusting' she shouted, pointing to the mirror
'Ah Honey,' sighed her mother, hugging her tightly, 'It's just a spot.'

*John Cobban*

## TRAVELLING IN TIME - A CYCLING DAYTRIP OF BARRA - 11TH SEPTEMBER 2001

Sudden pain, head throbbing, dizziness, made him hold the gate and then sit down. In St Barr's churchyard, fear, panic, death edged into first place. Coffee and cake, at Barra airport helped locate spirit of place. Finding planes then and there, being used as missiles in New York blew it.

*Robert D Shooter*

## A Mountainous Task

It was the highest climb he'd made. Up and up he went. He panicked when he saw the long descent. He toppled, fell head first, down and down, to his mother's arms.
'Again!' he squealed, 'again!' and ran back around to the ladder of the slide.

*Margaret Newbold*

## REALISATION

The room was icy cold and clammy. I had this sense of fear and foreboding and somehow felt trapped.

I groped my way along the walls fumbling for a door but alas there was no door.

But how could there be? I suddenly recalled I'd been dead for a hundred years.

*Amelia Crichton*

## WHEN THE END BECOMES A BEGINNING

Lost-love, disappointment, despair had wheedled him evilly to this clifftop climax.

Dark, befoamèd rocks below - compelling as a true-love's arms.
'Embrace me!' he cried, 'Let me forget!'

But jump he could not for Life held his arm and She whispered so warmly,
*'I can be less cruel.'*

***Julia M Glenn***

## WHY?

We watched mesmerised, as the air liner crashed into the tower. The explosion. The fire. The smoke. The carnage. The multi thousand lives. Then the dust, monstrous, engulfing the streets as the towers caved in, taking more lives. The wreckage. The heroism and determination of the emergency workers. The waiting?

*Leslie Holgate*

## FORGIVEN

Forgiven, mechanically
her hand grasped her captors
unspeakable joy filled her soul.

Arrested for hiding Jews
during Nazi occupation
standing before her in dreaded
uniform was captor who had her family
executed herself cruelly tortured
standing with outstretched hand
begging forgiveness.
Slowly her frozen trembling hand
took his, whispering forgiven brother.
Filled with God's love
blessed by cruel hand
that once tortured her.

*Frances Gibson*

## THE MAGICIAN

'Look!' said the magician and the air was filled with flowers.
'Look again!' he said and a beautiful lady flew about gathering them.

The child was enraptured. The magician waved his wand and flowers and lady disappeared. Except for one rose which fell into the hands of the wondering child.

*Margaret Rose Harris*

## CAREER LOST

Charlotte, a dedicated art teacher in a primary school, became depressed and was prescribed anti-depressants by her doctor. In the new year, the reception teacher fell downstairs and fractured her spine. She received a pension, bought a house and sued the school!

*Janet Eirwen*

## THE GIFT

'Happy birthday,' said his niece, giving him the package. I watched him impatiently open it.

'Thanks,' he mumbled uncaringly. I stared in shock at the cigarette case in his hand. In childhood I'd scratched my name inside. After many years, my late grandad, had sent it back, where it belonged.

*A Simpson*

# LEVEL CROSSING

He stopped his car near the station and looked round for somewhere
to park.
Just then his mobile rang.
'Darling,' came her voice 'I've missed the train.'
He dropped the phone.
Fuming he put the car into gear
and the speeding express took him half a mile down the track.

*D G W Garde*

## DRIVING TEST

Nervously, she started the engine, away she went onto the open road.

She tried to follow the coldly given instructions of the examiner. Remembered use of indicators and signs. Generally performed to the best of her ability.

Subsequently she failed but could honestly say she had made a valid attempt.

*S Mullinger*

## THE SOLAR SYSTEM DEFENCE INVENTION OFFICE

In the Solar System Defence Invention Office, I organised inventions, using my product marketing books. I marked pen illustrated, short science fiction stories and a solar system defence invention story. My published and unpublished stories were rewritten enlarged with a second part of each story; to create linked up stories.

*Ian K A Ferguson*

## PATIENCE IS A VIRTUE

Three men poised for action. Waiting as quiet and still as they could.
They'd watched all night for a sign, eyes straining in the moonlight.
Suddenly, one man noticed a ripple on the water. He rose silently,
reached out and pulled towards him - a 28lb carp.

*B Eyre*

## SPIRIT PIPE

'Alice where's me pipe?' Thirty years since you became Mrs Albert
Spear and you move my things and ignore me. When you talk to me
you always blubber. Ah! Me pipe's by that new vase with a lid on
mantleshelf Oh! What is written on the vase? Albert Spear 1926-1998.

*Phil Belcher*

## CULT CLEAVAGE

The invited chosen ones filled the selected venue. She was prepared for the ritual. Though the shining knife was sharp,
'Help her,' someone said.
A stronger hand over hers paused. A lightening brilliance blinded her. The room exploded in loud applause and cheering as the bridal pair cut the cake.

*A Cotter*

## No Leaks

As quaint as it was it still worked, its modern counterparts are much more flexible, designer, those flowing plastic stems, that throw away when finished look, nib like filters, holstered in the top left jacket pocket, leaking at both ends staining freshly laundered shirts, I'll stick with my clay pipe.

*Hugh Jackson*

## EAGLE

Sitting on a rock hard and cold by a stream running down the mountain, she studies her prey! Laying in wait all that longing to be free to express her heart. In a wilderness only one could enter her world. A flash of feathers ruffles her destiny. She spies him!

*Ann Joyce Farley*

## THE BEGINNING OF THE LONG JOURNEY HOME

Darkness enveloped the tunnel except for one distant light. The recesses in the walls loomed blackly, the traffic lights casting inky shadows as it thundered by, heart beating faster I neared the light, fear evaporating. Noisily the coach halted, thankfully I clambered aboard, relieved to be among chattering people again!

*Ruth Berry*

## LEGALISED THEFT

The thief stands in the corner, fully aware of the value of what he steals, knowing you will not stop him, he is bold, unafraid. As he speaks you laugh, cry, remember, forget, you hang on his word. The thief is TV, the valuable he steals is your life, beware.

*Geoffrey Woodhead*

## THE BIG ONE

He pulled and pulled, he could feel all the muscles in his body beginning to ache. He had to do it, no one would ever believe him if he didn't have the proof, camera at the ready he gave one last almighty tug. It was his, he'd caught - the big one.

*Pauline Nind*

## THE HOPEFUL FISHERMAN - AND HOW IT ALL ENDED

His fly cast, with rod and line, succulent bait falling on calm water.

A warm summer's evening.

The huge trout rose to the surface, mouth agape, caught the fly - well hooked!

Whereupon, struggle for supremacy ensued, our fisherman hauled in up to his armpits!

Who won? The fish, of course.

*Julia Eva Yeardye*

## EXODUS

The movement of people has been
Since the beginning of time.
Through the Red Sea they came
Across continents, across seas
Continually seeking grass greener
Or driven by some evil force to flee.
Walls will be pulled down
Barriers removed, and the flow
Of the human species will go forward.

*Joan Boswell*

## EYE WITNESS

The night was so hot I could not sleep. I heard our guest go downstairs, and following stealthily, I saw the glitter of his eyes as he crept through the moonlit house, and his crazed smile as he raised a carving knife and plunged it into the heart of a melon.

*V M Archer*

## LAZY DAYS

A punt glided slowly along the Oxford river, hugging the grassy bank and pushing aside the trailing willows. The sky was blue and birds sang on that lazy summer day. A youth lay in the punt, one hand trailing in the water leaving behind a crimson trail.

*Terry Daley*

## SUSAN AND BILLY

Susan and Billy were in love. They arranged for their parents to meet at Mum's home. One day Susan and Mum were waiting. In comes Billy and Dad. Mum screams, he's your dad. I divorced when you were two. You are half brother and sister. Kiss and be friends only!

*Kay Taylor*

## POWER

Works party, Xmas, mistletoe, mutual attraction, temptation in store room, stolen love regretted, guilt on both sides, constant chasing, ignoring, unanswered phone calls, morning sickness. Hospital scan positive, body swelling, anger. Constant rows, people talking behind backs, production figures down, much discontent, denial. Him wages clerk, her director, result dismissal.

*Robert Thompson*

## IF ONLY - (THOUGHTS AND WISHES)

I stared at the boot with an uncontrollable rush of excitement. It looked so warm and inviting, willing me to take it on, to experience its inner warmth. This is no ordinary boot you see, for this is Italy my garden of Europe, tempting me as always to her beautiful land!

*A Bodle*

## SEVEN YEARS OF PLENTY, SEVEN YEARS OF FAMINE

Jacob gave Joseph a coat of many colours; this and Joseph's dreams angered his brothers; they sold him to slavery.

His master's wife betrayed him. Imprisoned; but release came when he interpreted Pharaoh's dreams of plenty and famine.

Joseph made ruler, stored grain saving Egypt and his family from starvation.

*Alice Blackburn*

## THE PEEDIE MUGGIES

It was a cold day, a very cold day, the brass monkeys were playing football on the ice, it was thin ice. The ice ravens were waiting, the sun was their friend and encircled, the ice surrendered and consummated the B-monkeys. The icicles laughed till they wet themselves.

*John M Heddle*

# RUN OR SHOOT

Their victim hung chained to the wall.
'Run him through or I shoot you!'
His the rapier, hers the pistol.
His shoulders sagged, he half-turned, presented the blade,
saw the pistol waver, completed the turn and launched the sword,
she fell back in disbelief.
They were watching the rushes.

***Frank Ede***

## RUNAWAY

The train, driverless, hurtled towards the sun. Someone shouted
'Do something.'
I leapt from the carriage and hung onto the huge coal hopper. I
scrambled over with the wind in my face. It was frightening.

With the line disappearing beneath, I cleared the gap and landed on the
footplate. I was faced with a full set of taps and levers and the fire in my
face.

Just then I awoke, sweating. Just then my mother said 'Been dreaming
again, have you?'

*G Hodson*

# GIMMICK

It was late in the morning when the sun was finally persuaded to rise,
rinsing his gleaming teeth of fire with yours at the nasty slipstream of
memories, crushing angry passion flowers and wild berries among your
virgin forests to face the day like a man as he must without you . . . and
why must you be always so cold and serene like the distant stars? This
sunny day is like any other among the serenade of sorrows that remind
you of cold battles foregone and old soldiers deserted like nobody's
mundane business . . . it was late in the evening when all the bottles of
perfume finally rushed to woo you and your aroma and musk of
richness that made the sun go quietly down across the yonder rivers like
a dandy whimper . . . and so the sun must rise and the sun must set and
the sun must cry and wry its useless hands till you're aflame and nearly
all your rivers go all so blatantly dry

*Prasenjit Maiti*

## RESULT?

He felt himself grow hotter and hotter, beads of sweat creeping down his flushed cheeks. His legs began to weaken, he felt nauseous. His throat was dry, and he desperately tried to swallow.

In his sweaty hands, he clutched the envelope that held his future.

His GCSE results.

*Georgina Giles  (14)*

## A SPOOKY FIFTEEN MINUTES
*(True story)*

One fog-bound night, in isolated farmhouse kitchen, dairymaid and twin boys played I-spy. Parents had gone visiting. On hearing seemingly 'Phantom footsteps' ascending the stairs from the cellar below - the three huddled together!

Fortunately the parents returned, and on investigation the . . . 'Footsteps' were found playing cards slowly, slipping singly, from staircase shelf.

*Daisie Cecil-Clarke*

## THE BELL

The old bell had hung on the rafters for many a year, and was said to only ring as a warning of inherent danger. No one believed this old tale. Then one night the bell began peeling and the occupants of the house got out before the fire consumed everything.

*Duchess Newman*

## ON THE SURFACE OF IT

A mole puzzled by the 'knocking' above, up to the surface came. The blackbird was puzzled too - at what it saw, - which wasn't 'a worm' - like they both enjoyed. They looked at each other, and went on their way. Hoping to find, what they both wanted to eat that day.

*Bakewell Burt*

## THE UNBELIEVER

'I don't believe in God or hell,
You can keep your Bible!'
Scoffed the atheist.
They were sheltering in a haunted house.
The priest awoke, to hear his
Companion, cry out from his bed
During the night.
There is hell, and I'm in it!
His hand had burnt his Bible!

*A E Doney*

## ASTRONOMER

Three astronomers royal discovered a new star. It was a kind of comet. They decided to follow it to its source. It pulsed all day and night. The astronomers were puzzled. Would it be a breakthrough for science? A source of new life? A miracle? The star led to Bethlehem.

*Alan Pow*

## CLAIR DE LUNE

The waterwheel creaks in the moonlight dissolving as he lights his cigarro. Hearing sounds of splashing, his eyes slit in desire. The girl rises naked; puts a finger through the smoke ring he has kissed towards her. In perfect harmony they swim upstream. The Director shouts: *'Cut!* It's a wrap.'

*Michael Fenton*

## ARRIVAL AND DEPARTURE

I came.
I saw.
I conquered.
I left.

*Douglas Wood*

## NOT EVEN A 'GOODNIGHT'!

A stranger stopped me and pointing at our flat asked,
'Have you two girls just moved in?'
I nodded.
'It has a ghost you know, there's . . .' I cut him short,
'Don't tell me!' I shouted, 'I don't want to know!'

We could not afford another move and already our suspicions were
aroused. Lights were going off when switched on, files were found
thrown around in the office and others out of order. Once we heard
footsteps coming up the stairs. Already perturbed after one month!

The electricity was tested and passed.

We told no one! If it came to it, who would purchase, knowing?

Two sisters dined with us one evening and one excused herself to visit
the 'loo'. After some time she returned exclaiming 'You have a ghost!'
Before anyone could reply or question, she added, 'I put the light on
three times and each time it went off, and I was left sitting in the dark.
The last time I was absolutely terrified, so much so, tears were running
down my face and I prayed holding my cross with all my being, it
stayed on! Otherwise I would have run from the flat!'

As she spoke we all heard the Welsh table leaves flap-flap against the
legs. Twice! We stared at each other in disbelief, as someone or thing
must have bumped into it.

Without a word the sisters took off racing down the stairs and out of the
front door!

*Hilary Jill Robson*

## SPIRIT ABROAD

Did you hear that
No, what was it
I don't know
You go and see
*No*, you go
Oh, this is silly
I'll go . . . There I told you so
It was nothing
*Bang crash*
I thought you said it was nothing
*OK,* I lied
It could have been old Bert
Didn't he die in the well?
Yes, but that was a long time ago
It could have been him
You go,
*No,* it's your turn, I went last time
The door slowly opens
We look at each other . . . *Oh no*
In walks . . . yes, you guessed it
A cat, with flowers in its fur
Miaow

***Carole A Cleverdon***

# A LUXURY WEEKEND

The first prize in one of those well-known women's magazines was a luxury weekend in Lord What's-his-name's old and dilapidated, but, sumptuous castle in the wilds of nowhere.

Sara looked up from her new word processor and gazed at the twinkling lights showing through the trees in the growing dusk.

'Now let me see,' she murmured to herself 'that title and those twinkling lights have given me an idea for a story.'
She settled herself down with enough paper and began:

Sara and Peter decided to accept the prize they had won and drove off into the wilds where they were promised Lord What's-his-name would meet them and take them to the castle.

Arriving at an equally remote village where their car promptly broke down, they were dismayed to learn the Lord would not be there to take them on due to circumstances beyond the usual control and all that! However, after an hour waiting around a taxi driver dropped them by some steps in front of two of the biggest double doors they had ever seen and unloaded their bags beside them. The double doors opened slowly and they were met by a very old looking butler and an equally ancient housekeeper. Following them through to the hallway, they were lead up a magnificent flight of stairs to their room. Everything was dark and gloomy and covered in dust and cobwebs. Not a word was spoken as they shuffled up to the landing.
'Dinner at eight!' croaked the butler and seemed to disappear into the darkness along with the housekeeper and they were gone!

Peter walked over to the big window where Sara was gazing out over the trees in the darkness.
'What do you make of it so far?' he asked.
Sara looked puzzled.
'I'm not sure what to think,' she replied turning towards Peter. 'There seems to be something odd about the whole place. It's a feeling I've had ever since we came through those great doors, and those two that met us; they didn't seem real to me.'
Sara ran her fingers along the mantelpiece.

'Look at all the dust and cobwebs. What did you call the butler?'
Peter laughed, 'Creep!' he said.
'He certainly gave me the creeps,' Sara retorted, 'and the housekeeper looks as if she has been dead - for years.'
Peter turned to look through the window again.
'There seems to be a lot of activity going on among those trees,' he pointed. 'What on earth are all those lights?'
He pulled one of the curtains back. Sara moved back from the curtain and suddenly, 'Look out!' she shouted. An arrow smashed through the glass. 'It's an arrow!'
Peter leapt back. 'An arrow?' he exclaimed. 'What on earth are they playing at?'
A great roar of voices below the window followed by more arrows swishing in.
'Quick,' Sara shouted, 'let's get out of here.'
Grabbing everything and Peter's arm they dashed down the stairs to the double doors. Would they open? Peter jumped on the great handles and heaved. The doors suddenly moved. Tumbling down the steps they landed in a heap at the bottom. It was suddenly and strangely quiet. No shouting, no arrows, no lights. The taxi was still there too.
'Are you going back already?' he queried. 'Quick! Let's get back to the village!' Peter gasped, looking over his shoulder in disbelief. They clambered in and were off and flopped down in the plush seats with relief.

The taxi driver began rambling on about the remoteness of the castle as they made their way back. He was saying '- and they do say that this is the four hundredth anniversary of the storming of the castle in fifteen eighty-eight by a marauding rabble from the north.'
Sara and Peter looked at each other and 'swallowed uncomfortably'.

*Nelson Peters*

## PAINT OR BLOOD

It was a cold dark night and Angelica couldn't sleep. Climbing on her window sill she looked out across the houses, there was nothing there so she stared at the stars. She had done this many, many times before. Her attention turned towards the garages that ran perpendicular to next-door's garden. It suddenly seemed like daytime, even the trees behind the grey and blue buildings looked fresh and green. Then there were only the trees, as if she was seeing through the modern buildings. A new picture. Long grass, trees that bend and sway in the wind and a boy in old dingy rags playing catch. Up, up the ball goes towards the sky, then down into a tree. It's stuck, too high for him to reach so he begins to climb. Out onto the branch that holds his ball.

'No, don't!' she cries, 'the branch is going to break; you'll fall.'
She screams even louder. She wants to turn away but she can't. Snap: the branch breaks and the boy falls onto the spiked fence below. Then the picture fades and all is as it was. Angelica walks over to the spot where the boy fell the next day. There behind the garages on the rails that separate the buildings from the graveyard she sees a splattering of red paint that runs down the grey metal. Still the paint remains no matter how many times the rail is painted grey.

*A M Williamson*

## DRACULA'S DAY OFF

As everyone is aware, Dracula's castle lies in the area known as Transylvania, and it is not easy to find on a London street guide. However, Dracula had an 'off day', like we all have. You know, when you pick up a teapot and the handle falls off, that kind of thing.

On this particular day, he had just made it home, back to his padded coffin, before daylight lit up the mountain tops, so he was lucky not to have disappeared in a puff of smoke, if the sun's rays had caught him unawares.

On top of that, mice had built a nest in a corner of his coffin, and he had to get rid of them, before he could lie down in comfort. It was a day of disasters. The local butcher's boy had a puncture on his bike, and couldn't deliver some fresh liver Dracula had been waiting for, and when it began to rain heavily, the raindrops pattered on his coffin, and kept him awake. On top of that, the stonework on the castle battlements came crashing down into the courtyard below.

At last, night came, and Dracula could fly free to become the vampire he was.

It was only when he reached the nearest village, that he realised he had forgotten to bring his number one, best fangs with him . . .

*G Bannister*

## LATE CALLER

The door was closed upon the last of his guests, and he was alone in candlelight. He saw the remains of the evening, illuminated by the wavering flames that danced sensually on bookcase and mantelshelf, pale spectres of the night spent.

The Ouija board still lay on the floor where they'd all sat around it. He had always believed, in this overcrowded universe, there were no such things as ghosts. To prove this, he had invited his naïve, easily gulled friends, and challenged them to show him he'd been wrong in thinking the supernatural pure bunkum.

After several hours, and pages of garbled, meaningless 'messages' later, they had failed. Secure in his cynicism, he'd shown how those clinging to these childish beliefs deserved what was coming to them.

Actually, something was coming to him instead. He'd drained his final drink, and was about to close the window before sleep, when there came a rapid knocking at the door. It persisted, becoming more frenzied with each sharp rap. He tutted. Draped across the chair was a long dark coat, and though he didn't recall seeing it there before, obviously this was its owner come to retrieve it.

As he reached the door and drew back the bolt, a sudden gust of midnight billowed into the room and killed the candlelight, just as he opened to see who it was . . .

It's said they could hear his screams a mile away.

*Jonathan Goodwin*

## WHO CALLED ME?

It was a cold winter's morning and my alarm clock had just gone off, when I heard a loud crash. I jumped, got up and walked down a few steps and called 'Mum?'
There was no answer, as I walked down the last few steps I realised my heart was like a racing car. As I approached the living room I heard another crash! I jumped again and my legs turned to jelly. As I paced myself to walk through the living room, I saw that things were scattered along the floor. At the same time as I was walking into the kitchen I felt someone's eyes on me, I turned around quickly, no one was there, but I did however notice the back door was open. I went out into the garden and I had to fold my arms as it was so cold, I looked towards the back gate. It was swinging open. I ran to shut it. As I was running I heard someone call my name. I spun round but no one was there. I ran back towards the back door. When I reached it I took one last look around and went inside and shut the door behind me. I felt someone or something touch me. I screamed. As I turned, I saw a familiar face. It was my mum. She said 'Sorry.'
I said 'Did you call me?'
'No,' she said.
If it wasn't her, then who was it . . . ?

*Angela Anderson  (13)*

# A Job For Life

The cry was weak and plaintive.

'Help! Please help me.'

Pushing open the door, I went towards the bed. An old lady with wispy white hair was hunched up under a thin coverlet. Pale blue watery eyes looked at me from under heavy lids.

'Can I help?' I asked.

'I want Millie,' she said. Her voice showed no weariness now. 'Where is she?'

'I don't know, but I can find her for you.'

Her hand grasped my wrist. I was surprised by the strength in her skeletal fingers as she pulled me closer.

'I'm smarter than she thinks,' she said, nodding her frail head, *'and* she listens at doors. Millie knows I always have breakfast before ten o'clock. I'll have to have a word.' She nodded her head again and released my wrist. 'I must get up now but I will need help. I have a rehearsal after lunch,' she pointed a long finger at the wardrobe.

'I will be obliged if you would get my blue suit. Millie should be here; I pay her enough; she has a job for life. When I was on the stage I never had to remind her to put my clothes out. She organised everything.'

Tears began to slide down her wizened old cheeks.

I tiptoed away from the bed 'I'll find Millie for you.'

On the landing I spoke to the matron.

'The old lady in there' I began . . .

Matron stared, 'That room is empty,' she said, Miss Alicia died last year.'

*M Raw*

# ALONE

A leaf was spinning through the air: imitating a lover's dance as it was caught in the wind. It came to rest beside a hut. The windows were dark and desolate and the wind pushed against them trying to get inside. A crack was found and the wind entered, shifting the air within.

A dim bulb sprouted forth its offerings to life; casting shadows on the walls and highlighting a man sitting on a chair. An inch and a half of ash clung to his cigarette. The wind blew it away. His eyes were wide and searching. The wind teasingly played with his hair; causing his fringe to sway. It tickled his face but he couldn't scratch it. He hadn't been able to move for hours. It felt like someone was holding his head. He sat, terrified, watching the walls.

The shadows played there. Four of them. They looked like they were dancing. And they were holding weapons. These looked large and sharp. He could see no eyes but he knew they were looking at him. Minute by minute, step by step; they were coming closer. Their bulk slowly blocking the light.

Outside, a branch tapped against the windowpane and an owl spread its wings to drift to the moon. It paused at the top of a tree, cocking its head to one side to listen. It could hear a sound. A human sound. It was a scream. And it was getting louder.

*Sandra MacLean*

## A WANDERING RETURN

Wandering through the dark corridors, Edora stumbled upon a new door she could not open. Walking through it, she glanced at the bodies lying on the beds; living ghosts with faces more blanched by what life had shown them than anything supernatural.

She could not fully understand their pain for she had been numb since the accident. Fingering her swollen, disfigured face with a fragile hand, she sighed at the memory. That was her pain. Spurred on somehow by her own sadness and self pity, perhaps to drive it further into herself, she looked upon the perfect faces of the sleeping girls. Feeling brave tonight, she wandered into the ward, up to the first girl whose name marker read 'Dea Dayoure.'

Never again could she lie as did Dea and the others. Those days were long gone, and now she had her own private room of sorts. But it is lonely being alone, when solitude is so silent and so still, when no eyes look upon you and no faces appear before you to look upon. Edora lifted a trembling finger to her pale cheek, but there was no tear tracing its way down her face on its pitiful journey, a suicide mission as it dashed onto the hard floor, or onto her cold, quiet white neck. Her kind could not cry unless they had been doing so at The Time.

Sighing to herself, Edora rose and drifted back toward and through the locked door, to continue her eternal wandering.

*Helen Marshall*

# My Cycling Companion

As I cycled from the station on a bleak winter's evening, I was looking forward to a fireside supper, and bed. It was cold and damp, murky and moonless. Suddenly a shiver ran down my spine, someone was with me, watching me, eyeing my every moment. Another shiver, an awful foreboding, there was someone.

I speeded up, yet still this apprehensiveness. I took a look askance, and there he is. Another cyclist wheel to wheel, a shape, hooded, as I, pedal for pedal, beside me. A shape, a shadow, but not a shadow, a presence. Faster, faster, he too went faster, pedal for pedal, I slowed, he slowed. I moved over the road, pushing him onto the verge, then the hedge. Still he cycled pedal for pedal, wheel to wheel.

My heart pounded, thump, thump, thumping like mad, it must be a shadow, a reflection! But how on such a night. My mind was in turmoil. It can't be so! I took another glance, still there, a silent, shadowy vision, an apparition! Oh no, oh God!

The next minutes were frightening. I just rode and rode, harder and faster, with my head down, not looking, not hearing, scared as a rabbit. At the turnpike I swung left for home. Was he there, I glanced again, no sign, no shadow, no presence. Thank God. I tried to slow, my heart still pounding, I couldn't.

My mum said 'What's the matter, you seen a ghost?'
I didn't answer, I think I had.

*D Haskett-Jones*

## ANTE LUCEM (BEFORE LIGHT)

Fact or fiction - friend or foe
Created in a book - for all to know
high over a North Yorkshire fishing village
a ruined abbey - bewitched the horizon
faint ghostly chants - echo on Christmas Day
or is it only legend or myth as they say

By day he sleeps in his castle on high
by night he flies in the blackened sky
be it garlic - crucifix or wooden stake
with the count's kiss - it's your blood he'll take

So catch a glimpse of his silhouette by moonlight
but come the dawn - he'll have disappeared
Vampires - from the beyond - is where they come from
but can you honestly say you have met one

Let the cloak of darkness - haunt your sleeping hours
before the break of day - breaks the spell.

*David Charles*

## THE STORY - STRANGE EVENTS

The account begins - when the whole family decide they have a real need to pack up and be away from it all - we have left it late - summertime is coming to a close - all is settled - Cornwall is chosen - a small fishing village named Looe, even has its own island off the mainland. The arrangements have been made to enjoy our stay in a high position in St Martin's Lane - East Looe. The house has been in a family for some passing years, that has come to a finish. House is now in trust - let out - with rent received - placed in trust, caring for ones in real need. We settle in - say our first goodnights - morning arrives. At once the conversation begins.

'Did you hear that very strange sound?'

'Yes indeed - I believe I heard two voices - a name was called out with 'Are you there dear?'

There seems no peace this night - our house has been taken over by total strangers - we decided we were all tired out - just having passed thoughts and made plans for our day ahead - in truth - we are still on edge over events and ask locals, it comes to light - the owners had died together - and are convinced their spirit of life is in the house - didn't welcome strangers to share with them - they had both been killed when in a local church, a German war plane - had to unload its bombs. We decided we couldn't stay - another day - we packed, returned the keys and left it, to the ones that make a visit in the night.

*Rowland Patrick Scannell*

## WHERE THE GREY LADY

It's New Year's Eve in this middle haven,
In this quiet little village of Bishop Middleham,
Stories prevail, mainly from my mother's mouth,
As told, between Church Street and High Street,
Nearing 12am all drunks disappear,
To East, to West, to North, to South.
No one right now will come out,
Not one New Year's reveller will come near,
For Church Street and the school bank,
Icy owned, belong to her.
She floats, she slips and with her
She brings, death's icy nip,
In veils and icy winds she is blown,
In mists, tortured and icy cold,
Slowly every inch she'll grip,
This phantom grey glides down the road.
Her veils are blown in tails behind her,
Her icy lightened form, mysterious, defines her.
She's seen, she stalks, in repetitive steps displaced,
All people keep away, they say she has an evil face.
This lady is seen, at every eve of every year,
She gets to the top of the school bank,
Then she will disappear.
In snow, in frosts, in rain,
Year in year out, again and again,
When clocks strike midnight, 12am,
She returns from whence she came.
Then all Bishop Middlehamites, can celebrate,
Their, New Year again.

*Susan Carole Roberts*

## INKY BLACK FINGERS

Their back-packing holiday now drawing to a close, they drifted through happy memories of the past few days. As they strolled through the twilight hours into the realms of darkness, searching for their last night's resting place, off in the distance picked out in the fast fading light, Tom viewed an old crofter's cottage. The night was warm and humid, the haunting silence broken only by the crunch of dead leaves under foot echoing into the night, as they trod the winding path to the cottage. As Tom chewed uncaringly on a stalk of grass, Mandy sensed an eerie chill enveloping her, a chill that bit deep to her bones, tearing at the very fabric of her soul, moon-cast shadows haunted her every step closing in on her forever, stretching inky black fingers of the night grasping, clutching at her very being. The illusions of darkness devouring her every thought, trying to tear her away form the comfort of Tom. The haunting sound of silence, the whispering of the hedgerows seemingly beckoning her on, multiplied a thousand fold in her head, rising fear played tricks with her mind, unseen icy fingers pushing her on up the path to her forbidding shelter.

Mandy clutched Tom's hand tightly. Tom drew her back at a small fork in the path. After some thought he chose to the right, leading to a much larger building in a far off corner of the field. As they drew away from crofter's cottage Mandy felt herself being wrapped in a warming glow. The fears of the night fading away, leaving her bathed in her pleasant thoughts of her past few days with Tom. Her unexplained fears remain locked up in the little crofter's cottage, now just a ghost in her happy memories.

*B Wardle*

# MYSTICAL LOVE

For the first time in years the bed felt uncomfy, it was like lying on a gigantic concrete slab.

'Please not tonight!' She thought bouncing on the springless bed.

'Why can't things go right for me and Derrick?'

Reaching over to the sparkling crystal bowl Emily touched the smooth coated biscuits, and ran her fingers over their appealing flashy tops.

Picking one out she tried smelling it as she took a bite relaxing with the sweet taste that tickled her tongue, as she waited for Derrick to enter the room.

A harsh breeze blew the cotton curtains as her body chilled.

Hot air like steam appeared on exhalation, her mouth dry, and the biscuit feeling like a broken rock.

Mysteriously a damp, musty smell began lingering around the bedroom as she shivered.

'The Ghost of Belmora,' she gasped.

Emily suddenly stiffened like an icicle as the closed door began to rattle violently, and the handle turned.

She felt sick, the rocky biscuit became distasteful as her throat tightened. Spitting out the biscuit her eyes widened with fear.

'Derrick,' she screamed, 'Help me!'

Scrambled to the top of the bed she curled up like an embryo as the door slowly opened.

'Miss me my lady?' the bubbly spectre chuckled approaching.

Screaming she watched as he hovered over the bed, his eyes keen

'Oh my love!' He whispered, 'I've waited two hundred years for you!'

*Caroline Rowe*

## THIS ONE

Not up on trees, Andrew found out it was an ash. Devlin next door, being Irish, knew about trees.
'There's this one here and two further down.' 'It hypnotised your dad, especially later on when he was slowing.'
'Soothed him, I suppose.'
Andrew walked past this one daily, to and from the home where mother had been the last three months.
He'd never married. Just him and mum when dad died.
Devlin and his wife Mary had been neighbours for years, however.
Tonight, closing the gate, once again he heard;
'Why are you leaving her?'
Three months of looking up into the accusation and seeing only ash branches. Dad could keep mum buoyant but with him gone, Andrew had coped until upon mum's increasing immobility he'd reluctantly placed her in care.
'Why are you leaving her?'
He hadn't opened the bedroom window for three months.
Tonight was August-hot, so tired, maybe unwell with some vague virus, he'd opened it, falling asleep quickly enough.
Devlin watched the funeral quests driving off.
A week since Andrew died in sleep. Heart. Curtains still drawn next day at noon. Police came. Had to break in.
Only a few mourners, now all gone. Him and Mary with all the catering. He'd go help her wash up.
Turning from the gate, it sounded something like
'Why are you leaving her?'
Devlin looked up, wind in the branches, nothing but his nerves. Been a funny sort of week. Must see the doctor about these headaches though.

*Peter Asher*

# AFTER THE THIRD STILE

A sparkling Saturday.
Guy looked again at the map and directions he had cut out of the
newspaper from the Short Country Walks section.
A chance now for exercise in the fresh air - so he drove out near
Ravenroost Village.

He was able to park on the grass verge nearest the first x-marked stile,
because a Range Rover already there suddenly shot away.

The stile enabled Guy to walk alongside a wood. A second stile allowed
him into a pasture where curious cows followed him to a third stile.

He climbed into a large ploughed field in the midst of which he saw a
scarecrow wearing a dark hat, a dark overcoat and striped red and white
scarf.

'Get on to your mobile. Fast. 999. Tell police to follow a Land Rover
with two men in it. They've murdered Jerry Shaw. Tell them to send
someone along the Ravenroost Way. After the third stile . . . the
scarecrow . . . the scarecrow.'

Startled, Guy saw the speaker, a middle-aged man, wore the same hat,
coat and scarf as the scarecrow. Frantically, he dialled . . . the call over,
he saw the speaker had vanished.

With misgivings, he walked to the scarecrow. Horrified, he found a
corpse in those clothes lashed upright against two long sticks in the
form of a cross.

'Jerry Shaw?' he whispered.

A raven settled on the dead man's hat as it began to rain.

*C M Creedon*

# I SAW HER

I saw her standing by the gate,
stood 'neath the amber street light,
appearing to keep a vigil,
throughout the starlit night.
Her long, flowing hair,
glistened an angelic gold,
yet from where did she arrive,
amidst passed days of old.

Was my cottage her house!
For it's two hundred years old,
was it cruelly taken from her,
or was it so reluctantly sold,
I was never afraid to see her,
instead - a tear dampened my face,
I wished I could invite her in,
to chat afore the crackling fireplace.

I went to the local archives,
to see what I might find.
Alas this my lucky Tuesday,
fate to me was oh so kind,
I saw her name was Constance,
my cottage once her cherished nook,
until sixteen seventy four,
when their lives the plague had took.

Now I never see her.
Maybe I took the time
to cry and try understand her
and why fate took her in her prime.

*Steve Kettlewell*

# TROUBLE AT MILL

In 1993, I worked in an old mill. One Christmas Eve, I heard voices. I walked to the doors and went up to the third floor. A man and woman stood, inside a large room. She held a tool with a curved blade. I asked them what they were doing, but they just carried on talking.

The woman seemed to be taunting the man, who raised his hand. She shrank back, and tripped. I knew she had fallen on the blade. Her companion knelt down beside her. He turned to me, and said, 'Tell them I didn't do it.' I was about to reply I had seen it all, when the scene faded from view. I don't know how I made it back to my office. The receptionist said I must have fallen asleep. After the holiday, I made some enquiries. It transpires that, in 1902, a man, named John Ablethorpe, had been employed at the mill. He had become infatuated with a married woman, and she had sneaked out of her house on Christmas Eve, to visit John. Her husband had his suspicions, and had followed her. When he heard the raised voices, he burst through the doors to find, his wife dead in the arms of her lover. At the subsequent trial, Ablethorpe, was accused of murder. He admitted the quarrel, but maintained it was an accident. He was found guilty, and hanged at Manchester, still protesting his innocence.

The ghost was never seen again.

*William Tarbett*

# THE CHILDREN'S ROOM

There is a boy called 'Sam' who loves to explore.
Sam was looking at a house over the road, who ever he asked about the house said it was haunted.
Sam decided one night to go and explore this house so he went up to the rusty gate and opened it, then he was at the door.
He was about to knock when it opened, he turned on his torch and went inside. He saw a light upstairs and made his way up the dusty stairs, when he got to the top, the light had gone and in its place was a door and on the door were the words 'Children's Room' so he opened the door slowly and went inside.

It was dark but Sam could just make out that there were cots, rocking horse and toys all around the room. All of a sudden the lights came on in the room and the cots started rocking and the rocking horse rocked and the noises of children filled the room. Sam backed away to the door still looking around the room. The children started to sing, Sam made a grab for the handle and ran as fast as he could down the stairs.
He turned, there were footprints appearing in the dust but there was nobody there. Every night when he goes to bed, he hears the children singing and when he looks out of his window he sees little children waving at him and singing.

*Nicole Bates (13)*

# A DECEPTIVE NIGHT

The street became dark and eerie due to a street lamp that had expired, a figure at a neighbouring bedroom window hung motionless in the dimly-lit room, while in the shadowy street a parked car concealed a murky face looking towards me constantly and unflinching, I looked back to the hung figure at the window, searching for the slightest movement, but it remained completely still.

Returning my eyes to the parked car, the menacing face seemed to intensify his stare towards me.

Had I stumbled onto a macabre scenario? Was the hanging figure the helpless victim of the stranger in the car? Had I raised his suspicions that I might be a witness to his evil transgression?

Filled with fear, I closed my curtains sharply, imagining he might spy his chance to get me also. I bolted the doors and locked the windows before I nervously went to bed.

The following day I had some appointments to keep, I was pretty tired when I returned home that night. Deciding to have an early night in bed, I was about to draw the curtains, then chanced to look up at the bedroom window of the hanging figure and then the suspiciously parked car, still outside. And then I laughed and laughed as I saw that the hanging figure was a dress hung at the window and the face in the car was simply a headrest. Fortunately, one of my appointments that day was for a new pair of spectacles from the optician's.

*Gemini Cherry*

# WITCHING HOUR

. . . Lost and alone in the Witching Hour, your spirits sink as though devoured, but as shrewd enchantments weave their most subtle glamour, the Incubus come calling . . .

Do you lie in fear of the Evil One, the Prince of Darkness and Devil-Spawn, Master of Legions and deception - or William Blake's Red Dragon? The composition is most rude though simple - Lucifer: the Lord of Evil, rampant in ascendancy over a vanquished angel - the simple principles of imago interpretation.

Entirely nefarious this 'Dance Macabre'; unsound agents cavorting so beneath the stars, foul and fetid as best they are, aching with lewd desires. So have a care should witches pass, for not all possess broomsticks and dark hissing cats, though before the moon will they dance and laugh, seeking fresh corruptions.

'Short is the way, and quick, that out of light leads down to hell'. That's quite some line, though wise as well. Demons you see aren't crude of sight, they recognise their salvation. So in the dark and damp wild unsound places, they ply their art behind hooded faces, clad in robes of purple with eyes wild and blazing do their serve their Lord's foul abominations. For they possess no fear of the Holy One, neither in God's might nor anyone - you cannot dispel them with a gun, but where they lead you'll follow!

So as the night finally yields to day, and as the witches slyly slip away, let us pause to ponder where they might stay, these most subtle foxes. For they're all around but we can never know, for sorcery does itself rarely show, they lurk in the shadows until the glow-worm shows; with patience how like an ambush. So snuggle down within your bed, draw those covers tightly about your head, and breathe real shallow to hide your dread - and perhaps you'll see the morning!

*Sam*

# THE PHARAOH'S DAUGHTER

It was very hot and sweaty as usual but it was a week or two before they got to some empty booby-trapped rooms. But Dick and his team were the ones not to give up. They had plenty of time and went on into the third week. Dick made a small hole and couldn't believe his eyes. There in the middle of the room was the tomb and around it was lots of treasure. Dick was the first to enter. It was so quiet, it was as if they were taken back in time. Dick saw the amazing Golden Eagle, he went to pick it up.

'Don't touch,' said his colleague.

'It is cursed, you'll have to kiss the mummy to break the curse,' cried another.

'Rubbish,' said Dick. It was beautiful and heavy. Made of solid gold.

It took the team another week. Everything was shipped to a museum in Spain.

It was time to go home and, as promised, he married his sweetheart, Sandy. As the years went by all his friends had children. Dick and Sandy were happily married but were missing children. One day as Dick was going through his paperwork he came across the pictures of Egypt and then remembered about the curse. That's it! He knew he was cursed. He had to fly to Spain to kiss the mummy to break the curse.

The following year they conceived their first child.

*A Bhambra*

## THE CLOCK'S TICKING

Tick, tick, tick. Time was passing and her life wasn't moving. She wasn't sure what time he was coming. A shadow came beneath the door, while she was sitting. Hurriedly, she opened it. No signs of him. Beside the pile of garbage, she spotted a glimpse of eyes. It hid. She felt that someone was watching her from a distance. Her unborn child started to move inside her. Pains started to build. More, even more. Minutes later, it stopped. She sat and waited again.

She felt uncomfortable just by sitting, she walked around while looking out of the window, and saw a huge white dog appear from the pile of garbage. It stopped for a while, then looked at her. Seconds later, it vanished towards the dark passage.

Tick, tick, tick. She heard the sound of the clock that never stopped. It was almost midnight. No sign of him. She decided to retire to her bedroom, but she left her bedroom window slightly open. She noticed an eye of a small dark creature peeping through the window. She opened the window, but the creature on the other side of the wall ran inside the broken tunnel that had been lying over there for years.

The silence was interrupted by the sound of an old clock. It was ticking again. *Tick, tick, tick.* 'Why did it stop for a while?' she asked herself. Moments later, she heard the creaking sound of their old wooden door.

Finally, her breathing returned to normal.

*Angelita Redfern*

# OLD CROW

It sat perched on the damp ashes of her love letters. Already nine days had passed since the demise of 'that romantic old fluff'. At least that is how Tom pictured his mother. How he yearned to have her back now but it was too late; or so it seemed.

'I can't believe she's dead,' he cried, pushing the bed sheets aside. It was 6am. Total darkness . . .

The bed was tucked in a convenient space inside the kitchen flat. Tom knelt over and peered under the bed.

'Mother, are you there?' He played with his fears imagining her rotting corpse lying under him, releasing a sick stench. How sick . . . it certainly wasn't the Tom his mother had known.

'Mother, those love letters . . . I should never have destroyed them. But you must realise I had to. Oh never mind!'

The kitchen curtains were never drawn. They projected the moonlight onto Tom's face. Tonight he was restless. He opened the fridge door and browsed around. His eyes lit up a wine bottle.

'Caaw . . . Caaw.'

'What the hell!' He shuffled to his feet and plodded wearily to the window. It still sat perched on the ashes of her love letters. As long as it stayed put, Tom didn't mind the old crow. But wasn't it odd that a stuffy old bird, black as night, should sit in solitude, caawing every night?

'Mother would have shot you. That's why I won't.'

Returning to the fridge, he uncorked the bottle with his long fingernails. It dripped all over his chest. But what dripped wasn't wine. It was blood! 'All right Tom, just take it easy old boy. You're still under shock. That romantic old fluff is taunting you. Go back to bed quietly.' Consoling himself, he lay down, humming.

'Hum . . . hummm . . . hmmmm . . . mmmmm . . .' Bees?

Tom swerved around to find a hornet perched on the wall.

'I hate you Tom . . . I hate you Tom. Rot in hell!'

Suddenly it wasn't there.

'Caaw! Caaw!' It was the old crow.

Tom shuffled to his feet again, upset. His stomach stiffened and a jet of blood trickled out from his belly button. 'W-what's happening? Am I cracking?'

It was 6.30am. The dimming moonlight tempted Tom to peer outside to catch sight of the crow; that was not difficult. The darn thing never moved an inch. But why was it perched there, on her love letters?

'It's not there. It's . . . not there!' Now Tom really was scared. Overcome with giddiness, he fought back. 'M-must . . . resist . . . mustn't fall down.' But the forces of evil were bent on destruction tonight of all nights. Nine days to the night. Nine days since Mother vowed to come back for her beloved son. It was then that the crow appeared before him . . . and for the first time, revealed its putrefied face.

'Nighty-night, Tom.'
'Aaahhh! The hauntmare begins.'

*Rajeev Bhargava*

# CANDLE IN THE RAIN

Suddenly she was awake.

She heard rain pattering on the tent, but not as loud as her heartbeat.

'Wake up.'

He didn't move, so she shook him. Usually he was a light sleeper, but she couldn't wake him. She tried to whisper in his ear.

She couldn't find his head.

Panic. She fumbled for the torch, crying. It's just a practical joke, just one of his bloody jokes . . .

A light. A flickering light. A candle. His body. No head. She screamed, but no sound. Just the pattering rain, just her heartbeat.

I'm dreaming, I'm dreaming, I'm dreaming.

The candle floated away. No hand.

Suddenly calm, she thought, well, if that's the logic of the dream, I'll go with it.

Into the rain. The candle never spluttered, but she felt the rain on her body. She giggled. Here I am following a phantom candle in my bra and knickers. She became frightened again.

She tripped, rolled over sharp rocks, fell through air, plunged into water, sank, surfaced, heard laughter, sank, struggled to free her legs, held her breath until she had to gulp, heard water rushing through her head, felt terror to the exclusion of everything, saw a candle growing, growing, going out.

Suddenly she was awake.

She heard rain pattering on the tent, but not as loud as her heartbeat.

'Wake up.'

He didn't move, so she shook him. She tried to whisper in his ear. She couldn't find his head.

Panic.

*Fred Brown*

# TIME

She gave one last glance around the empty rooms then gently drew the front door closed. It was the end of an era but she and Dave had discussed it a long time before the parting.
'You should find somewhere smaller for yourself, release the capital on this place, start to enjoy life,' he joked. 'You know me, a stack of jazz records and a good sound system and I'm fine.'

The parting had been heartbreaking at first, the unbearable stillness replacing the noise of his music flooding the house. The uncomprehending look he gave when she complained of the whiskey and cigarettes. Yet afterwards she craved for their scent even shutting herself into his wardrobe, anything to bring him back, closer to her . . .

At first his friends had visited wearing hangdog expressions, fishing for sympathetic words, all the time thinking,
'God, I'm glad it wasn't me.'

Today was the day: a clean break with the past. Dave would have loved the cottage, the ideal retirement home, complete with summerhouse where she could escape from the incessant music.

She drew up in a quiet country lane, glad to have arrived before the removal men. The key in the lock felt unfamiliar, awkward, but she finally triumphed.
'A good clean and polish then it will look more like home.'

Then she heard it, subdued yet insistent, the unmistakable sound of Dave Brubeck's Take Five. She smiled and ran into the empty room.

*Barbara Holden*

# THE HOMECOMING

It was a cold wintry night, Sue could hear the wind howling through the trees like a wolf calling to his pack and there was a constant tapping on the window from the tree branches outside. Sue was alone at home studying for her 'A Levels', her parents were dining out with friends.

Sue was sitting at the dining table with her back to the coal fire which illuminated the whole room, giving it a rosy glow and filling the room with warmth. On one side of the fireplace there was a rocking chair which was rarely used but sometimes mysteriously rocked to and fro as if an invisible being was seated there. The only sound inside the room was the tick-tock of the grandfather clock, which was standing in the far corner, like a sentry on guard at the Palace.

The hours had passed quickly with Sue painstakingly studying the contents of her books, sometimes being interrupted by a flash of lightning falling towards Mother Earth. The clock struck twelve and suddenly Sue had a strange feeling that she was not alone, it was as if someone's eyes were boring a hole in her back and she could hear the movement of the rocking chair. Imagine Sue's surprise when she saw a little old lady, dressed in black Edwardian style, rocking back and forth and smiling happily just as if she had returned to her rightful place in the home. It was Great Grandmother Bella returning to her favourite chair!

*Maureen E Wood*

## MURDER AT THE RED BARN

I had chosen this country hideaway to come to a decision. Which one to choose - Debonair Derek, the extrovert, charming companion (but being honest with myself - an effort to keep up with), or Faithful Fred, my childhood sweetheart, quiet, reliable and a shoulder to cry on?

Which did I want?

As I tossed and turned in bed it didn't help me that the farmer had told me this place was haunted by the ghost of a young stable lad who literally lost his head. The farmer's wayward daughter was discovered frolicking with the lad in the hayloft of the Red Barn. In his rage the farmer lunged at the lad with a pitchfork pinning him to the ground through his neck. Blood spurted out everywhere and his head was severed.

The story upset me so much I couldn't rest and a compelling urge forced me to creep downstairs, to cross the cobbled yard and push open the creaking barn door. As I did so my foot struck something round, soft and squashy which in the dim light looked deep red. I screamed and fled back to bed!

In the morning, thinking it had all been a bad dream, I ventured to the Red Barn. I slowly pushed open the door but it was wedged by something. With an extra heave it gave way and there strewn about was an upturned basket of blood-red beetroots.

I have had enough excitement, so I know who to choose.
I need the safe shoulder of my Faithful Fred!

*Olive Miller*

## PETE'S PARAGLIDING PAL

Pete's paragliding parachute snapped and crackled above him as he ran down the slope and flung himself into space. The crag, from which he had launched himself, loomed over the valley with its sandy floor stretching to the sea two miles away. The breeze swirled, disturbing the upward surge. Pete dipped towards the valley floor, aiming for the sand bordering the river.

Suddenly a flash of purple and pink shot across his flight path. Pete cursed, swerving violently.
'What the blazes was that?'
A figure in a purple jumpsuit hung from a pink gliding 'chute off to his right. The figure dipped towards him once more. Pete swore as he wrestled with his control lines, trying to avoid the inevitable collision. He hit the lower slope of the rocky hillside that bordered the valley and rolled downhill entangled in his parachute.

A shepherd ran to help open the silken parcel.
'You alright?' he asked.
Pete gasped for breath.
'Yes. Did you see that idiot who flew across me?'
The shepherd looked puzzled.
'No,' he said. 'I didn't see anyone else. I was thinking you were lucky to land here and not down there.'
He gestured towards the valley floor.
'They pulled a lad like you out of there last week. Too late though, he'd drowned in the quicksand. The helicopter pulled him out. Shocking pink his parachute was, with his body hanging from it like a burst balloon. All limp and purple!'

*Fred Mayers*

## BANNOCKBURN

A call to arms came from the uncrowned king - answered by a common army of thousands. On a hot midsummer day the assembled clans faced the great English army. With blood, sweat and sacrifice, the Scots fought with bravery against tyranny and oppression and finally gained their freedom.

*Philip Wade*

# THE DAY THE WORLD NEARLY ENDED FOR HARRY

Everything went smoothly until noon.
Then the meandering stream flooded homes;
The sky turned puce and gale-force winds lifted roofs
                                    and felled mighty oaks.
Seconds later the sleepy village scene was just a memory.
Harry stared in disbelief.
His favourite screen-saver had been devoured - by a computer bug!

*Betty Lightfoot*

## C'EST LA VIE

Above.
The pounding of the guns,
Below.
The pounding of his heart,
Then . . . silence.
Sat inside his trench.
Heart still pounding,
He stood upright.
He fell back.
On his face no shock.
On his lips no breath.
His heart now still.
The trench,
Once his saviour, now his lonely solace.

**Charles David Jenkins**

## THE TERROR

She closed her eyes and screamed. The lights were unbearable and she felt herself slipping into terror, thrashing out as they held her. Their cold hands and eyes pierced her humanity as surely as their steely instruments. Groping for comfort, she found her unresponsive, drugged. 'It's a girl!' they said.

*Anita Layland*

## THE LION'S TALE

On safari in Kenya one day a hunter rode a horse, a golden mare. When he was confronted by a lion he calmed this beast simply by saying, Steady, Metro, steady.

His fellow hunter was quite surprised and asked how his friend knew the lion's name was 'Metro'.

'As you can see,' said the lion tamer, 'I'm riding a golden mare and everyone knows the Metro Goldwyn Mayer lion.'

*Charles Meacher*

## A MOST POWERFUL FORCE MADE ITS WAY TOWARDS US

Very slowly at first it crept forwards getting more powerful with each movement. It slithered towards us gathering speed and gaining height, whilst others followed closely behind. With baited breath we waited. Till finally the wave arrived breaking and crashing on the shore.

*Christina B Cox*

# OUT OF THE MIST

I woke to a morning of swirling mist, like grey cotton wool, blanketing all sound and muffling the noise of the distant, slowly moving traffic. It was some time since I had walked in the park, but somehow, on this grey November morning, I felt oddly drawn to do so.

Skeletal trees stood like limp grey ghosts on either side of the park gates and frosted grass bordered the whitened paths.

Clusters of vivid Rowan berries seemed to burst through the mist. Thrust out, like offerings of ripe fruit, from the bare, cold fingered branches of the tree. Their strident red contrasting starkly with the dove-grey of the morning. I heard a movement, a rustling in the bushes and glimpsed a bedraggled squirrel foraging for acorns. A startled blackbird pecking the sparse remains of an apple core chittered angrily and darted for cover.

There was no movement on the pond, the water fowl all hidden from view. Willow trees hung like hazy curtains, trailing their fringed branches in the water, and over the island, the mist swirled slowly like steam rising from a kettle on the boil.

On a mound, where the ground rose slightly to the Manor House, a circle of hawthorn trees stood poised like a hovering coven of witches. I held my breath, half expecting them to move, slowly gyrate and dance within their circle. Feeling a little spooked, I started violently as a large dog came bounding out of the mist. Thoughts of Sherlock Holmes and the Hound of the Baskervilles flashed through my startled mind. The dog jumped up at me, placing large, muddy paws on my shoulders, nuzzling my neck and depositing warm, wet licks on my cold face. I rubbed his ears and neck, while we both expressed pleasure at having encountered one another.

It was then that his owner emerged from the mist, nodding a curt 'Good morning'.

The spell was broken. Now becoming painfully aware the frost had penetrated my fingers and toes with its cold, nagging ache.

I headed for home, my mind firmly focused on a cup of steaming hot coffee, with perhaps a little 'dash of something' on which to warm my icy fingers - and of course - the cockles of my heart.

*Hilda Jones*

## Twixt Life And Death

Beneath the cold black earth, she stirred.
The waiting was over.

The primeval passions that lay deep
within her, sought the warmth her
naked limbs so desperately needed

Escaping the bonds of darkness, she
clawed her way to the light.
Where she grew and flowered, into a
thing of beauty.

*Jim Cuthbert*

## GRANNY'S SECRET

The gravestone read 'She rests in Peace, a life lived to the full' Jasmin Joannah Joynston - 1910-1967.

Born in Leeds, the youngest of thirteen children, Jasmin Jo as her friends called her, was the prettiest child in town. When she was three she was the Pears soap baby for the new-style hoardings that were becoming popular in shops and on gable ends of streets. Her mother was thrilled as they were paid a considerable sum just to allow her to be photographed. Unfortunately her mother never saw the money, which she had hoped would buy shoes and clothing for her children. Their father took it and squandered it on drink and horses.

By the time Jasmin Jo was twelve she was a real beauty with flame-red ringlets and the brightest green eyes. All of her brothers and sisters, those who had survived, were working and she attended school most days. Education was not thought necessary for girls but her mother insisted this child would neither go down the mine nor into the factories as her other children had.

At fourteen tragedy struck the family. A house fire killed all but Jasmin Jo and Bernard. They, having no living relatives, went to live with a neighbour whose children had grown up and emigrated. It was thought that Jasmin Jo and Bernard would be their replacement family.

Life was bleak with no mother to tell her troubles to. Jas, as the man of the house called her, was very unhappy. He had taken an unnatural interest in her, she being so young and he so old, but still he continued to do 'things' with her and made her promise that it was to be their secret. If she told of their secret she would be damned. This continued even when she gained employment as a housemaid and only had short breaks at weekends.

By the time she was seventeen Jas found herself with child, and turned to her employer for help. The kindly family took her in and promised to look after her and her baby. It was much later that she realised that she had been truly 'taken in' and never suspected their motive. After the birth of the baby and when she had fully recovered, it was decided that her bedroom should be redecorated. She was at first thrilled until she saw the lavishly brash way in which it was done. The foolish girl thought it wonderful until the night of her first man caller.

Pensively she waited, her benefactors had said that she was to entertain a guest staying at friends nearby. The man came and went, then another, day after day, her life as a prostitute continued until she was twenty-nine when the old man died. His wife, not wanting to give up the luxurious life she had become accustomed to, proposed to Jas that she take over the business. After all, a beautiful woman with outstanding features and an aptitude that became her profession, would be a natural. A large bedroom was partitioned off to make two, and two girls were employed.

After a year or so they moved to an even larger house and more girls were employed, by now Jas had become an accepted socialite with a discreet income and very influential men friends. One in particular was Jack Fearon. He owned a public house and supplied all the necessary requirements that gentlemen like when calling upon her ladies. It was after all a social club for men.

Over the years, Jack took a firmer hold on the business and when the old lady died and left the property to Jas, they continued in their businesses together, bought a bigger and better property in a more affluent part of town and extensively modernised both house and garden.

When alone Jas would often reflect upon the fate of her young son. He had been taken from her at birth and she had never seen nor heard from him since. Jack was her rock when she, depressed and lonely, turned to him in despair. But, as often as he proposed marriage to her, she remained unwilling.

One morning a young man walked into the house and asked to speak to Jasmin Joannah Joynston. Suspicious of his enquiries and afraid she may be arrested owing to some controversial complaints about the 'goings on' in the house, she told him that Jasmin was no longer in her employ and asked if she could pass on a message to her if she saw her.

'Just tell her that her son came to visit and would like to meet her!'

Her heart missed a beat, this strong good-looking young man was her son. He left the house and said he'd return. That evening she sat, pondering what to do. She'd write a note, no, she'd say she had gone away - no - can't do that, I said I'd pass on a message. Would he understand the truth?

On her deathbed she lay, her son, his wife and her grandchild. A smile on her still attractive face, though hair now silvered, it still shone.
'Are you sad, Granny?' the child asked.
'No, my dear, I have had a good life since your daddy found me and I have no regrets,' replied Jasmin Jo.

She slid silently away during her sleep, her daughter-in-law and granddaughter no wiser of her torrid past.

*Marjorie Briggs*

# A NIGHTMARE IN FRANCE

It was a loud howl that first woke me this morning. I hadn't been sleeping very well at night in this strange bed anyway. This was to be my last night here. Usually the heat kept me awake, and when I did fall asleep I had one nightmare after another. All paranoid reworkings of the events of the day, or of my plans for the next day. I felt vulnerable here, in this mobile home - I'd have hated to think what I would have been like in a tent!

The howl continued. It sounded like a hurt animal - a dog or wolf or something. I didn't even know if they had wolves in the French countryside. I turned over and tried to sleep. It was only two in the morning and I'd only been in bed for a couple of hours. Funny how when you need to sleep, you can't! The thought of the six hour drive to the ferry made me force myself to relax my breathing and I nodded off again.

The howl was somehow sadder this time as I woke again from my restless sleep. I was sweating under the thick layers of my sleeping bag. I would be cold if I got out of bed with clothes this damp. The duration of the drawl was getting longer as the animal continued to whine away. I considered getting up to investigate. It sounded quite near and I'm a sucker for animals, but it was still dark and I was afraid of the dark.

I was afraid of a lot of things. My nightmares were subconscious evidence of this.

The first night I had dreamt that my son had gone off on the campsite by himself and had got lost. I woke up screaming for him, waking my son and husband from their peaceful slumber.

The next night I dreamt that I was dragged from the French countryside road that I had taken to jogging on every day. I woke up fighting my faceless assailant, and kicking my husband awake too.

On day three of our holiday, the weather turned cold and I woke the next night dreaming that we couldn't get out of the mobile home because it had been buried under eight feet of snow. I was shivering in the cold night air as I had kicked the covers off and was only wearing a T-shirt.

The circus had then come to the campsite grounds the next day. They passed me by as I was out jogging, and like most French vehicles aimed to run me off the road. Shame I'm not a cyclist, they give them a wide berth. They obviously don't think much of runners in France. My nightmares that night were all circus related. In my first nightmare I had been kidnapped after they had run me over while I was out jogging and placed in a display cabinet as the 'flattened woman'. The only recognisable part of me was my Nike trainers. My son noticed this and said to his dad, as they looked at the circus display, 'Look Dad, she's got the same trainers as Mum!' They laughed at this. I woke up screaming, 'It's meee!'

I fell asleep again right away, and went right back into a circus dream again. This time I found myself falling off tightropes that you had to walk to gain entry to the circus. Ironically, I didn't even go to the circus. My family went without me as I have always been against the circus because of the captive animals - you can't impress this on a four year old however, and my husband obliged.

The howling got worse. It was still dark out. Andy was sound asleep beside me, oblivious to the painful whines. I went back to sleep.

'Mummy I'm scared,' Declan was sleepily saying as he woke me to squeeze between his father and I. 'Sad dog crying,' he said as he snuggled into sleep. This time the howl was more of a whimpering. The sound that a hurt dog would make. I could no longer stand it. My mind was filled with images of a hurt dog - maybe escaped from the cruel circus owner. It had probably been badly beaten and had managed to escape. Maybe it was now at death's door and I felt guilty that I hadn't been brave enough to investigate sooner. If it dies, it would be all my fault because I hadn't gone out sooner.

It was light now. Five-past five. I slipped out of the bed and into my flip-flops. I pulled my fleece over my pyjamas (as it was still cold out - adverse weather conditions the newspapers reported) and I went out to investigate.

'Howwwl! Howwwl!' There it was again. I turned over in my bed, pulling the covers around me. 'Hmmm!' it whined. I shivered. My covers were being pulled from me. I opened my eyes slowly against the brightness of the sun that now lit the room. My eyes focused on my husband who was tightly holding Declan's face in against him. What now? Have I scared them awake again with screaming in my nightmares? My husband backed against the wall. I sat up and pulled the covers back on me and to tell them that I'm OK now. I'm awake now! Surely they should be comforting me? As I looked down I didn't understand why I was looking at hair covered limbs that were not legs anymore. I thought I was saying this, but instead, I howled and howled and howled!

*Anita Nelson*